NICK JR.

# GO DIEGO GO!™

## Phonics Reading Program

# Let's Go Rescue!

GW00786352

• Baby Jaguar Can! • Out of the Nest • Quick! Help the Fish!
• Hop Like a Tree Frog! • Stuck in the Mud • Time to Sleep

## SCHOLASTIC INC.

New York   Toronto   London   Auckland   Sydney
Mexico City   New Delhi   Hong Kong   Buenos Aires

Designed by Kim Brown

Go, Diego, Go!™: Baby Jaguar Can! (0-439-91305-5) © 2007 Viacom International Inc.
Go, Diego, Go!™: Out of the Nest (0-439-91306-3) © 2007 Viacom International Inc.
Go, Diego, Go!™: Quick! Help the Fish! (0-439-91307-1) © 2007 Viacom International Inc.
Go, Diego, Go!™: Hop Like a Tree Frog (0-439-91308-X) © 2007 Viacom International Inc.
Go, Diego, Go!™: Stuck in the Mud (0-439-91309-8) © 2007 Viacom International Inc.
Go, Diego, Go!™: Time to Sleep (0-439-91310-1) © 2007 Viacom International Inc.

ISBN-13: 978-0-439-93229-5
ISBN-10: 0-439-93229-7

12 11 10 9 8 7 6 5 4 3 2                                           7 8 9 10 11/0

Printed in the U.S.A.
This compilation edition first printing, February 2007

elcome to the **Go, Diego, Go!** Phonics Reading Program!

arning to read is so important for your child's success in school and in life.
ow **Diego** is here to help your child learn important phonics skills.

onics is the fundamental skill of knowing that the letters we read represent the
unds we hear and say. **Diego** helps your child LEARN to read and LOVE to read!

re's how these readers work:

➡ At first you may want to read the story to your child.

➡ Then read together by taking turns line by line or page by page.

➡ Encourage your child to read the story independently.

➡ Look for all the words that have the sound being featured in
the reader. Read them over and over again.

holastic has been encouraging young readers for more than 80 years.
ank you for letting us help you support your beginning reader.

Happy reading,

Francie Alexander
Chief Academic Officer, Scholastic Inc.

In this story, you can learn all about the short "a" sound. Here are some words to sound out.

**can    clap    past    grab    fast    that**

These are words that you will see in this story and many other stories. You will want to learn them as well.

**him    he    jump    to    you**

These are some more challenging words that you will see in this story.

**jaguar        climb        mountain**
**blowing       high         hooray**

GO NICK JR
DiEGO
GO!™

onics Reading Program

Book 1
short a

# Baby Jaguar Can!

by Quinlan B. Lee

**Can** Baby **Jaguar** climb
to the top of the mountain?
Let's climb with him
and Mommy **Jaguar**!
**Grab** the zip cord
and **clap** your hands.
*Clap, clap, clap!*

The wind is blowing **fast**.
*Crash!*
Oh, no! A tree fell on
the **path**.
How **can** we get **past** it?

We **can** swing on this vine.
We **can** swing **past** the tree.
But how **can** the **jaguars**
get **past** the tree?

**Jaguars** are **cats that can** jump high.
They **can** jump **past** the tree.
**Can** you jump like a **jaguar**?
**Stand** up and jump!

**Can** you see Baby **Jaguar**?
**Jaguars can** blend in well.
Look for **tan** and **brown**.
**Can** you find him?
No, **that** is a bird.

There he is!

**Jaguars can** run **fast**.

**Can** you run **fast**, too?

**Stand** up and run!

Run **fast**, **fast**, **fast**!

Baby **Jaguar**, jump to
the top!
You **can** do it!
Let's **clap** and say,
"You **can** do it!"
*Clap, clap, clap!*

Baby **Jaguar can** get to the top! Hooray!

In this story, you can learn all about the short "e" sound. Here are some words to sound out.

**help**   **egg**   **check**   **nest**   **fell**   **yes**

These are words that you will see in this story and many other stories. You will want to learn them as well.

**four**   **two**   **they**   **no**   **from**

These are some more challenging words that you will see in this story.

**toucans**       **tropic**       **crocodile**
**another**       **build**        **leave**

# Out of the Nest

by Quinlan B. Lee

The toucans need **help**!
They had four **eggs**
in their **nest**.
One, two, three.
Oh, no! An **egg fell** from the
**nest**!

**Check next** to those rocks.
Is there an **egg**? **Yes!**
Is it a toucan **egg**?
**Let's check**.

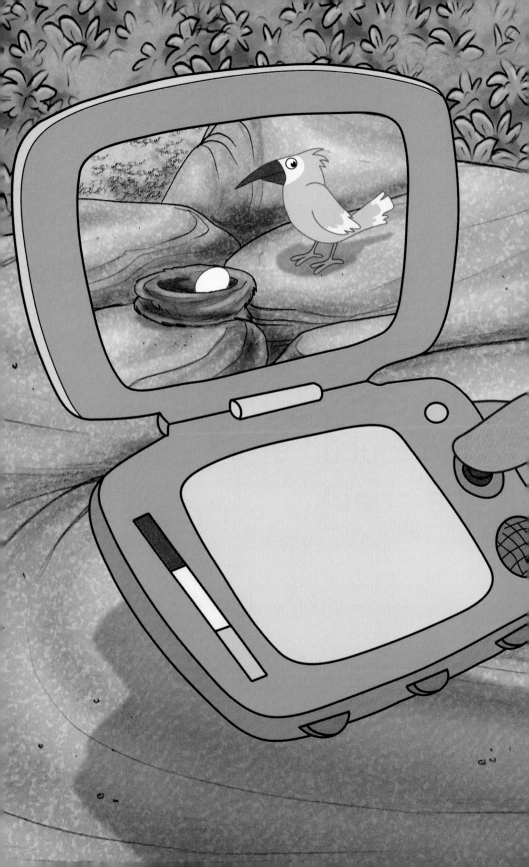

Toucans make **nests** in trees, not **next** to rocks. A **red**-billed tropic bird makes **nests next** to rocks. It is her **egg**.

**Check next** to the lake.
Is there an **egg**? **Yes!**
Is it a toucan **egg**?
**Let's check!**

Crocodiles make **nests** **next** to lakes.
This **egg** is a crocodile **egg**.
It is **best** to leave it alone.

There is another **egg**.
It is **next** to that tree.
Is it a toucan **egg**?
**Let's check!**

**Yes**! Toucans build **nests** in trees.
Toco, here is your **egg**.
Now you can put it back in your **nest**.

We did it! Now the **eggs** are in the **nest**.

In this story, you can learn all about the short "i" sound. Here are some words to sound out.

**ship**   **skin**   **snip**   **fish**   **fin**   **gills**

These are words that you will see in this story and many other stories. You will want to learn them as well.

**we**   **on**   **about**   **find**   **hard**

These are some more challenging words that you will see in this story.

**learn**          **trouble**          **coral**
**breathe**        **water**            **stretch**

NICK JR.

GO DIEGO GO!

Phonics Reading Program

Book 3
short i

# Quick! Help the Fish!

by Quinlan B. Lee

We are on a **ship**
to learn about **fish**.
A **fish is in** trouble.
**Quick**, **Click**! Help us
find **it**.

**It is** a frog **fish**.
Frog **fish** are hard to see.
Their **skin** blends **in with**
the coral.
Look! His **fin is** stuck **in**
a net.
We need to **snip** the net.

How **will** we breathe
**in** the water?
**Fish** use their **gills**.
We need something
like **fish gills** so we can
**swim in** the water.

Rescue Pack can help!
He can turn **into** an air tank.
Now we can breathe like
we have **fish gills**.
**Quick**! We need to help
the **fish**.

**Fish swim with** their **fins.** Let's **swim** to the **fish. Quick**! Stretch out your hands and **swim, swim, swim**!

Do you see the frog **fish**?
**His skin** blends **in**.
**His fin is** stuck **in** the net.
He cannot **snip** the net to
get free.

How can we **snip** the net?
**Clippers**!
Let's **snip with** the
**clippers**.
**Snip, snip, snip**!

We **did it**! Look at the **fish swim**!

In this story, you can learn all about the short "o" sound. Here are some words to sound out.

**frog    stop    hop    log    drop    top**

These are words that you will see in this story and many other stories. You will want to learn them as well.

**our    are    going    must    have**

These are some more challenging words that you will see in this story.

**river          coconut          pyramid
gloves          climb            jaguar**

GO NICK JR DIEGO GO!™

Phonics Reading Program

Book 4
short o

# Hop Like a Tree Frog!

by Quinlan B. Lee

The red-eyed tree **frogs**
need our help!
The **frogs** are **on** a **log**
going down the river.
The **log** will **not stop**.

The wind is making the ChaCha Coconut Trees **drop** their coconuts. **Hop** like a tree **frog** so they will **not drop on** us! **Hop, hop, hop!**

Do you **spot** the tree **frogs**?
There they are!
We must **stop** the **log**!
It is going into the pyramid.

Do you **spot** the door?
Look! It is at the **top**.
How can we get to the **top**?
I have gloves that stick
like tree **frog** toes.

We can climb to the **top**
like a tree **frog**.
**Hop on**, Baby Jaguar.
Let's climb to the
**top, top, top**!

Now do you **spot** the
tree **frogs**?
Quick! We must **stop**
the **log**.
We do **not** have a **lot**
of time!

Tree **frogs**, **hop** off your **log**
to the **top** of this **rock**.
**Hop, hop, hop!**
**Hop** to this **rock**!

We **got** the tree **frogs**!

In this story, you can learn all about the short "u" sound. Here are some words to sound out.

**yummy**  **stuck**  **up**  **but**  **mud**  **hum**

These are words that you will see in this story and many other stories. You will want to learn them as well.

**in**    **it**    **or**    **is**    **have**

These are some more challenging words that you will see in this story.

**llama**         **basket**          **mountain**
**fair**          **where**           **stretch**

GO NICK JR.
DiEGO GO!

Book 5
short u

Phonics Reading Program

# Stuck in the Mud

by Quinlan B. Lee

Linda the Llama has
a basket of **yummy** food.
She is taking it
**up** the mountain and
to the fair.
**But** she is **stuck** in
the **mud**!

Where is Linda?
Llamas like to **hum**.
Let's **hum** like a llama
so Linda can find **us**.
**Hum, hum, hum**!

I hear Linda **hum**.

Which path leads to Linda?

Yes! Let's go **up** that path.

**Hum** so Linda can hear **us**.

**Hum, hum, hum**!

We found her!
**Yuck**! This **muck** is sticky.
Let's help Linda
get **unstuck** from the **mud**.

We did it!
**But** now the rope is **stuck**!
Is it **stuck** in the **mud** or
**up** in the tree?

How can we reach **up**
in the tree?
Llamas have long necks.
Stretch like a llama.
**Up, up, up**!

We did it!
We got Linda **unstuck**
from the **mud**
and made it **up** to the fair
with the **yummy** food.

**Yum!** This food is great!

In this story, you can learn all about the long "e" sound. Here are some words to sound out.

**see**    **leaf**    **green**    **need**    **beak**    **sleep**

These are words that you will see in this story and many other stories. You will want to learn them as well.

**the**        **do**        **six**        **that**        **who**

These are some more challenging words that you will see in this story.

**animals**            **flashlight**            **toucan**
**something**          **upside down**          **sloth**

GO NICK JR DIEGO GO! ™

Phonics Reading Program

Book 6
long e

# Time to Sleep

by Quinlan B. Lee

The sun is not up yet.
Let's **see** which animals
are still **sleeping**.

We **need** my flashlight to
**see** in that **tree**.
What do you **see** under
that **leaf**?
Do you **see** a **beak**?

Who do you **see**?
It is a toucan.
Is **he sleeping**?
Yes! Toucans **sleep** at night.

Do you **see** something **green** under that **leaf**? There are six **feet**. Whose **feet** are they?

I **see three tree** frogs.
They have six **feet**
and six red eyes.
They are not **sleeping**.
**Tree** frogs **sleep** in the day.

Did you **see**
something **peek** at us?
I **see** upside-down legs.
Who hangs upside down
in **trees**?

It is Sammy the Sloth.
He **sleeps** in the day
like the **tree** frogs.
Now I **see** the sun!
Do you know what that
**means**?

Good morning, toucans!
**Sleep** tight, Sammy and
**tree** frogs.